TOBY TUCKER

Keeping Sneaky Secrets

Also by Val Wilding

Toby Tucker: Dodging the Donkey Doo

Toby Tucker: Sludging through a Sewer

Toby Tucker: Mucking about with Monkeys

Toby Tucker: Picking People's Pockets

Toby Tucker: Hogging all the Pig Swill

TOBY TUCKER

Keeping Sneaky Secrets

VAL WILDING

Illustrated by Michael Broad

EGMONT

For Jane Clarke – a great travelling companion.

Thanks for sharing Egypt with me.

EGMONT
We bring stories to life

Published in Great Britain 2007
by Egmont UK Limited
239 Kensington High Street, London W8 6SA

Text copyright © 2007 Val Wilding
Cover and illustrations copyright © 2007 Michael Broad

The moral rights of the author and illustrator have been asserted

ISBN 978 1 4052 1840 5

1 3 5 7 9 10 8 6 4 2

A CIP catalogue record for this title is available
from the British Library

Printed and bound in Great Britain by the CPI Group

Toby Tucker couldn't believe his eyes. Such a huge room! And it was just for him! The pink fairy wallpaper was a bit of a no-no, but otherwise, it was great.

THUMP! THUMP! THUMP! Toby stepped on to the landing and leaned over the banister to see what the racket was. 'Can I help?'

Don rested a heavy wooden chest against his knees. He took a deep breath and blew out. 'You can give me a hand with this, lad,' he said. 'What have you got in it? Dinosaur bones?'

Toby grinned. 'There's not much, really. It's the box that's heavy, not what's in it.'

They dragged the chest upstairs and across Toby's room, making tracks in the deep red carpet. Don pulled a face. 'Evie won't like that,' he said. 'It's new.'

Toby looked up. 'New? Did you buy the carpet for me?'

'Sort of,' said Don. 'We've only just moved in ourselves, so we had to buy a few bits. This house is almost as new for us as it is for you.' He wiped his hand across his sweaty brow. 'And we wanted you to have a nice room, seeing as how it's your first proper home. Like it?'

'It's brilliant,' said Toby. 'But, er . . .'

Don grinned. 'I know – the fairies. Don't worry, we'll get that sorted before you have any mates

2

up here.'

Toby knew that would be a while. New room plus new home plus new school plus new town. That all added up to no mates. Yet.

Light footsteps pattered up the stairs, and Evie appeared with a tray of tea, hot buttered toast and strawberry jam. 'Like your room?' she asked. 'Jeepers creepers, Don!' she said, before Toby had a chance to reply. 'What have you been doing to the carpet? Sledging on it?'

'Sorry,' said Toby, worried that he'd done wrong on the first day of his new life with Don and Evie Allen. 'It's my chest that did it. The people at the children's home gave it to me when I left. They said there's only a load of torn paper in it, but it belongs to me, so I have to have it.'

Don grinned. 'You're a bit of a mystery, you are, Toby Tucker,' he said, handing mugs round. 'No past – no record of you at all at the home.'

'That's right.' Evie sprayed toast crumbs as she spoke. 'And you could tell the staff think it's weird, too. Where did you come from, Toby Tucker?'

Toby didn't know what to say, but Don jumped up and said, 'Doesn't matter where he comes from – he can be the boy from nowhere as far as I'm concerned. The important thing is that he's here now, we're his foster parents, and we're going to get on like . . . like . . .'

'A house on fire?' suggested Evie.

'Birds in a nest?' suggested Toby.

'Pigs in a pigpen!' said Don.

Toby Tucker sat back on his heels and looked round the room. His clothes were in the white-painted wardrobe. Everything else was in a tall built-in cupboard, which had far too many shelves for his few possessions. Good-luck cards from the kids and staff at the home stood on the windowsill, and all that was left was the heavy wooden chest. It stood on the floor beneath the window. Evie said it would make a handy extra seat.

4

Toby lifted the lid and stared at the mass of torn paper. He plunged his hands into it and tossed the pieces into the air.

'What am I supposed to do with this?' he wondered.

Again, he plunged his hands deep into the chest, but this time he caught his little finger on something.

'Yowch!' He sucked his nail, then burrowed through the paper to see what he'd stubbed his finger on. It was an old wooden photo frame.

Toby gazed at the photo. The face meant nothing to him, yet it was a gentle face, with a smile that made Toby feel warm inside.

He turned the photo over. There was some writing on the back, in pencil. Toby looked closely. His eyes widened when he caught sight of his own name. He tilted it so the light fell on it, then read, his lips moving as he made out the faded words.

> The paper in the chest is your family tree. I wonder which little baby tore it up, eh, Toby Tucker? Piece it together and you'll find out who you are and when you come from.
>
> Gee.

He got it wrong, thought Toby. He meant 'where you come from', not 'when'.

Just then, Don yelled, 'Dinner, Toby! Your first chance to suffer Evie's cooking – ouch!' Laughter echoed up the stairs.

I'm going to like it here, Toby thought. He took one more look at the photo as he put it back in the box.

'Perhaps you're my great-grandfather, or

something,' he said to the gentle face. 'I hope you are. Were.'

After dinner, which Toby thought was ace, he showed Evie and Don his family tree. They were fascinated.

'If you can piece it together,' said Evie, 'you'll find out who you are.'

That's what the note said, Toby remembered. He didn't mention it though. Having a secret made him feel special.

Don pulled open a drawer. 'Here,' he said. 'No time like the present.' He handed Toby a roll of sticky tape. 'Want some help?'

'No!' Toby said quickly. 'Sorry, I'm not being rude, but I'd like to do this myself.'

'Of course you would,' Evie said with a smile. 'Hey! Maybe if you finish it, you'll be able to use it to track down some real family.'

'Yeah!' said Don. 'Like a second cousin three times removed, or something.'

'You might be a prince!' Evie bobbed a curtsy.

'Or a gypsy boy!' said Don. 'Cool!'

Toby grinned. 'Don't be daft. I just want to find out who I am!'

'Then you'd better get started,' said Evie. 'You have a quest. Who's Toby Tucker?'

Toby took a heap of paper scraps from the chest and dumped them in the middle of the carpet.

He worked at the family tree for ages. None of the pieces of paper fitted together. He found bits of names: 'Ro' and 'abeth' and 'rcus' and 'andra', and bits that didn't look like parts of names he'd ever heard of: 'illes' and 'Idome' and 'smond' and 'vieva'. And what was this one? 'ti'? What name could that be part of? Tilly? Tinker?

Don popped upstairs and put a mug of hot chocolate on the bedside table. 'Going to take a break?' he asked.

'OK,' said Toby. 'No, wait . . . This jaggedy bit . . . I saw another like that. Where is it?'

'I'll leave you to it,' said Don. 'Don't wear your eyes out.' He left, closing the door behind him.

Toby searched for the other jaggedy bit of paper. 'There it is!' he said. 'Let's see if they fit together.'

'Se . . . ti . . .' muttered Toby. 'Seti . . .'

He jerked his head back as a drawing appeared beside the name 'Seti' – a drawing of a boy in a skirt, with a head that was nearly bald.

'Wow!' said Toby. 'What's this? Invisible ink?' Then he looked closer. The drawing was changing. It was turning into –

'Me!' said Toby. 'It's me! What on earth...?'

Just as quickly, the drawing turned back into the boy with the bald head. As it did so, it shimmered with a silvery light.

The silvery light grew and grew. Before he had a chance to get out of the way Toby felt it touch him, then pass through him. It was like when cold jelly slipped down his throat, but all over his body. Toby trembled. What was happening? He was almost afraid to turn to see what had happened to the column of light.

But he did turn. And he nearly toppled backwards in surprise. Standing in front of the chest was – the boy in the skirt!

Toby found his voice. 'Hey!' he said.

Why didn't the boy turn round?

Toby got up and spoke again. 'Hey! You!'

The boy didn't move. Toby was narked now.
He took a step towards him.

Suddenly he felt himself being pulled forward, as if the boy was a giant, powerful magnet.

'Woah!' he cried, afraid he'd crash into the
boy and they'd both go through the window.

'Watch out!'

But there was no crash. A split second later, Toby found himself standing where the boy had been. He just had time to realise that not only had the chest disappeared, but . . .

'I'm wearing a skirt!' he cried as the room seemed to spin around him. 'What's happening to me?' As everything whirled and became a blur, he felt himself falling.

'Oooof!' Toby landed face down on the floor. He stretched out his hands. The thick red carpet was gone! Squidging through his fingers was sand – hot, yellow sand.

His head felt peculiar. His thoughts were muddled. 'I don't know who I am . . .' he thought. 'The sun's burning me . . . Sun? In my bedroom?'

A weird feeling washed through his body. He felt as if nothing was right – his thoughts tumbled and twisted and made no sense. Nothing made sense.

'Where am I? Who am I?'

All he was aware of was sand and sun. Hot sun. He knelt, and stayed on all fours for a moment.

'Oh,' he said slowly. 'Of course. I remember. I'm on my way to the river. And I know – I know who I am.'

He shook his head to clear it.

'I am Seti. And I don't like the look of that scorpion.'

60th year of the reign of Pharaoh Ramesses II

I wish there wasn't a single chicken in Egypt. If I had my way I'd send the whole lot back to Asia where they came from. Hardly anybody else keeps them. No wonder!

Our rotten cockerel, Nasty, went straight for my ankles this morning, as

13

usual. I didn't see him coming. Next moment I was face down in the dust, with fifty chickens scrabbling over me.

My white kilt! Why can't we stick to ducks and geese?

Is it any wonder I'd do anything to get off the farm? I help a lot, especially now it's shemu, the harvest season. Soon I'll give up school and work full-time with Father. When he dies and goes to the afterlife, the farm will be mine to worry about. Father says if I made more effort, I'd love it as much as he does.

Pish! I'll never love farming. But I'm stuck with it. And it makes me ill, I know it does. Today, after Nasty attacked me, I was on my way down to the river when I felt peculiar and suddenly found myself on my hands and knees in the sand.

When my head cleared, I leapt up smartly because there was a scorpion right under my nose. It looked almost as mean as Nasty. But it wasn't the scorpion that bothered me. It was me.

It's hard to explain, but for a moment I didn't feel like me. I had this ... this ... all-alone-in-the-world feeling, and I hated it.

I raced home, still feeling odd. 'You're not all alone,' I muttered to myself. 'You're Seti, and you've got a family, and they love you.'

I feel better tonight. More like myself. What happened today was weird, though. For a few moments, it felt like I was two people. One so terribly alone – and me.

School tomorrow, thank the gods – a whole morning off work.

School, and I was in trouble straight off for being late because Tiya followed me. The first I knew was when she jumped on my back. There I was, flat on the track, and grubby before the day started. No question about feeling weird today. Everything's completely normal! I took Tiya home, then ran to school like a wild bull. Luckily the master was in a good mood, so my punishment was just ink-making.

I made red ink for the master, from earthy ochre. Then I made black, using soot and water. I like using charcoal best. When you grind it, you

get a great crunching sound that really annoys the others.

We practised hieratic writing all morning. The older boys have started learning hieroglyphs.

Hieratic writing's quicker, because you can do it joined-up.

'Pick up your pens,' the master droned. 'Begin.' He sighed. 'Neb, how many times? Begin on the right.'

Neb's my cousin. He's left-handed and gets muddled because the master makes him write with his right hand. He'd be better off with hieroglyphs. You can write those in any direction.

Today we wrote on limestone flakes, called ostraca. I got a really smooth ostracon, so my writing looked extra good.

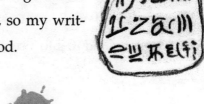

Next lesson was mathematics. I'm useless, but I tried to look interested. The master believes our ears are on our backs, so that when we're beaten, we listen.

I'll leave next year. Neb will leave, too. Then we'll have a problem. At school we can be friends. But outside school it's different. We're forbidden, on pain of the beating to end all beatings, to have anything to do with each other.

No school today. I had to deliver two geese to Uncle Wadj. Dead ones, luckily.

I love going to Uncle Wadj's papyrus factory and seeing paper being made. But first I went to the cave.

The cave belongs to me and Neb. It's where we meet. Nobody else knows about it. It's a short walk from my farm, on the hill above Neb's village. The entrance is hidden by a massive yellow boulder. You'd walk past without realising you could slip behind it, into a cooool cave.

I waited, but Neb didn't come. He was probably over on the west bank of the river, working
with his father – my Uncle Mose. Lucky devil.

I gave up and left. I'd been pottering along
for ages before I suddenly remembered I should
be carrying something. I raced back to the cave.
By the time I'd brushed the ants off, the geese
looked as good as ever.

My uncle was busy, so I watched the paper
makers for a bit.

By the time Uncle Wadj appeared, there was
a cloud of flies round the geese – and me.

'Seti!' he cried. 'How's my lovely sister?'

Uncle Wadj is Mother's brother.

'And how are those two idiots, your father and his brother Mose?' he asked. 'Still behaving like dopey hippopotamuses?'

I nodded. 'I can't ever remember them speaking. Neb and I are still secret friends.'

'They'll sort themselves out one day,' said jolly Uncle Wadj.

I gave him all my family news, and he gave me his. Then I said, 'I'd better go now,' and turned to leave.

'Seti? The geese?'

I'd forgotten them! I laughed and handed them over.

'Thanks,' he said. 'I wish you'd keep the flies!'

Harvesting's well under way now, so I don't go to school much. I helped cut barley today. Father says I'm old enough to use the sickle, but if today's

effort is anything to go by, that's a joke. I kept slashing towards my legs, instead of away from them. The workers could hardly bear to watch me. I'll probably chop my legs off one day.

Afterwards, I took some barley to an old widow friend of ours, and bumped into Neb. We quickly arranged to meet in the cave as soon as I'd finished.

When I eventually slid behind the yellow rock, Neb held something out to show me. 'Look,' he breathed, eyes wide, 'aren't these beautiful? I think one of the gods must have turned into a great white bird and visited our cave.'

I didn't like to tell him the feathers he'd found were from two dead geese.

'I'll put them in our treasure box,' he said, digging in the sand with a long sharp stone.

Neb and I have to share everything we've got with our brothers and sis-ters, which is unfair. When we discovered we'd both got something highly secret that we did-n't want anyone else to see, we made a treasure box out of reeds. We keep it buried in our cave.

I could smell that Neb had been working. His father – my Uncle Mose – is an embalmer at the Beautiful House, where they make mummies. Neb hates his work. He hates it as much as I hate farming.

He's mad. I'd give anything to learn how to

prepare people for the afterlife. Embalming bodies – making mummies – is important. If you embalm someone's body really well, they can be almost sure of reaching the afterlife safely. Do it badly, and they can be damned for eternity.

If I plant a few seeds too deeply, it makes no difference to anybody. How I'd love to be a mummy maker. But I'm doomed to being a farmer.

｜ᴗ｜⊖｜⊙｜－｜

Father let me go to school today. Afterwards, Neb and I went to the river with some other boys. They don't know anything about the family feud. Nor do Neb and I! We haven't a clue what started it.

Crocodiles have been seen lately, so we didn't swim. Instead, we went bird-hunting in the marshy river edges. We've been doing it for about two years. Neither of us has ever caught a thing.

We could net birds if we wanted, but that doesn't need any skill. We use throw sticks. It's harder, but it's more fun. Mind you, there's not

much skill in clouting your friend on the back of the head with your throw stick, as I did today.

Neb asked what we're up to on the farm.

I groaned. 'I shouldn't really be here. It takes weeks to get all the harvest in. Everything's ripening, so it's work, work, work.'

'Don't you love it, though,' he said, 'when all the hard work you've done – well, that Uncle Pepy and his workers have done! – when it turns into golden wheat, and fat onions and juicy melons?'

'No, I don't! It means bending, stretching and lifting for weeks on end,' I said.

'All my work gets buried in a tomb,' Neb grumbled. 'No one ever sees it.'

'Pish!' I said. 'Anyone can grow a cucumber or pick a fig. But not just anyone can prepare a dead body so it lasts for all eternity.'

Neb snorted. 'Who'd want to! Some of the things we do are so disgusting . . .'

He made a sicking-up sound, as if he was choking. He wasn't mucking about – that's what his work does to him. It almost makes him throw up. I can't understand it. He should face a heap of pig poo first thing in the morning. That'd make anyone sick.

Neb stood up. 'Better go. Father's expecting me.'

'Me, too,' I said. 'We're picking flax. I hate it – it gets up my nose.'

'If we didn't have flax, we wouldn't have linen,' Neb said. 'We'd have to wear animal skins or go naked.'

Pompous ass. Linen's linen. Linen's boring.

Although they say the royal family's linen is so fine you can almost see through it. Whoo!

'It's funny,' said Neb, and he wasn't smiling, 'I'd rather go to work on your farm, and it sounds as if you'd rather make mummies.'

'Mmm.' I had one last throw with my stick, and missed. 'Pity we can't swap places.'

Neb laughed.

I stepped carefully into the forest of reeds to fetch my stick. Not carefully enough.

You're supposed to be able to break a bird's neck with a throw stick. I'm more likely to break my own!

Later

I didn't pick flax. Instead I fetched fish from the boy in the market, then spent all afternoon being a donkey. The wheat was being cut so fast that the donkeys couldn't carry it all uphill. Everyone had to help.

I had a better time in the market. If you stand around someone's mat for long enough, being friendly, they usually give you something to eat. Today I got a pomegranate. I made a hole in the skin and sucked the juice out. When I'd finished I aimed the pomegranate at a dog peeing on a pile of cabbages.

'Thanks, Seti!' cried the vegetable seller. I left before he offered me a free onion.

Now the sun's going down, and Baba's crying non-stop. I'm on the roof – it's cooler here – and I'm making a clay dog for Tiya.

On the way to school today, I took a huge jar of honey to the brick maker. He's baking some mud bricks for Father, so we can repair some walls.

Brickmaking looks easy.

Father told me to come straight home. He gets in a state about this time of year. He's worried the akhet season will come early. (It never does.) Akhet's when the river floods for weeks on end. We must get the ripe crops, fruit and vegetables gathered in before then.

During the flood, our house is safe on high ground but our farm's underwater!

When Father was younger, he had to leave us with Mother for almost the whole flood season.

To pay part of his taxes to Pharaoh, he
went away, helping build temples or
tombs. Now he's older he doesn't work
as many days for Pharaoh, so he's home
some of the time, looking after the animals –
especially his rotten chickens. We've had
chickens in Egypt for a couple of hundred
years, and they've never caught on, but
Father's convinced they'll become popular. He
believes one day all farms will have hens running
round.

They're mad if they do. I hate
them. Especially Nasty.

Next day

Today's supposed to be a holiday. Hah! Farmers
never really get a break. Still, because I've worked
so hard, Father gave me the afternoon off.

But first, there was threshing. Groan! Why
me? All the stalks we harvested were spread out

on the ground. I walked the cows round and round so they trod on the stalks and broke off the heads of grain. They're the bits we want. It's good exercise for the cows, but hard work for me, pulling them along. They don't like me and if I had my way, I wouldn't keep them. I like the cheese we make from their milk, but that's about all.

Once I was free, I went to the river, hoping to see Neb. Good timing! He'd just got there. We went to our favourite inlet, which is too shallow for hippos. It's reedy, which I think is safest because if a crocodile pushes through reeds, you can see them moving. Father says nowhere's safe from crocodiles. We always make sure someone else is further out in the water than us, then they'll be eaten first and we'll have time to run.

I lay back in the water, the sun shining through my screwed-up eyelids. Neb stayed on his front, keeping an eye out for danger. Once I'd cooled off, I said, 'Neb, you know you want to be a farmer, and I want to be a mummy maker? And I said it's a pity we can't swap places?'

'Yes.'

'Well, it is, isn't it?'

'What?'

'A pity.'

Neb rolled on to his back. I flipped over and rested my chin on my hands, watching for crocs.

'What are you on about?' he said.

I took a deep breath. Unfortunately, my elbows had sunk in the soft sand and I got a mouthful of river. When I'd finished spluttering, I said, 'We can't swap places, obviously . . .'

'Obviously.'

'But we could teach each other. I could teach you farming, and you could teach me mummy-making.'

Neb thought. Then he said, 'What's the point? We have to follow our fathers' occupations, worse luck.'

He was right. But did it have to be like that?

'Hoy! What about when I own our farm?' I said. 'I could sell it and be a mummy maker. I'd easily earn enough to look after my family.'

'What about me?' Neb asked. 'What could I do?'

To be honest, I'd only seen a way out for myself. But I'm a quick thinker. 'I thought of that,' I lied. 'Just suppose,' I said – slowly, because the thought was forming as I spoke – 'just suppose, when we're grown up and our fathers have gone . . .'

'To the afterlife.'

I squished a sandfly. 'Suppose you and your family came to live in our farmhouse – we'd have to make it bigger, but I could do that. Suppose that happened. You could do the farming, and I could go mummy-making every day.'

Neb brightened. 'And when the flood came, I could go off building great temples for Pharaoh, and you'd look after both our families!'

I nodded. 'Let's do it! Let's make a solemn pact to help each other do what we really want to do.'

Neb frowned. 'But suppose our fathers live to be forty? Or fifty? Or even as old as Pharaoh?'

That was scary. This is the sixtieth year of Pharaoh's reign!

'If they do live till they're ancient,' I said, 'we'll be grown up. We could be brave and tell them we don't want to do what they do – and what we really *do* want to do.'

'All right,' said Neb. 'Let's make a pact.'

I laughed. 'What? Lying in the river?' I got up. 'Come with me.'

We were sun-dried by the time we reached

the cave. I dug up the box, and took out our most treasured possessions: our scarab amulets – our lucky charms. Mine's made of turquoise and Neb's is made of lapis lazuli. Real scarab beetles roll animal dung into a ball and push it along the ground. Ugh. I've seen them do it.

'This is our pact,' I said. 'I swear to teach you how to farm, and you swear to teach me mummy-making.' I held out my scarab. 'Let's swap amulets to show we trust each other, and we'll always be friends.'

Neb gave me his lapis lazuli scarab, and I gave him my turquoise one. When we put them back, everything in the box looked the same as before. It felt different, though.

As I walked home, I squinted at the sky and thought of Khepri, the scarab god. Just as the scarab beetle pushes its ball of dung, so Khepri was rolling the sun across the sky towards the west.

When I got back I had to shift a load of donkey dung.

I haven't seen Neb for ten days – a whole week! It's been work, work, work all day. The Nile will soon be rising, so it's hurry, hurry, hurry with the harvest!

The flax, wheat and barley are in, and threshing's almost over. I was so fed up today when I had to help Mother with the winnowing.

It's a dusty job, and you need a good wash afterwards, especially when Tiya helps.

In my opinion, winnowing is women's work. But Father says I must experience everything.

'How can you tell your workers what to do,' he asks, 'if you don't know how to do it yourself?'

Threshing – done! Winnowing – done! Today we tipped the final baskets of grain into our store. Mother took the last lot to make bread for us to share with the workers. She makes great bread, but we can tell when she's grumpy – all we get is hard, flat loaves.

Mother makes barley beer too. She puts chunks of half-cooked bread in water and leaves

it to ferment – Tiya says it goes bubble-ubble-ubble. When all the bits are strained out, it's ready! We like honey in our beer, but Father likes his spiced.

Uncle Wadj likes wine. We send him grapes, and in return he sends Mother something pretty to wear round her neck. His servants tread on the grapes, squishing the juice out. It ferments like beer. I hope they strain it. Imagine finding a sliver of toenail in your wine!

We started picking fruit and veg a week ago, and today Father let me go to school for a change. I'm way behind everyone except other farmers' sons. Never mind, I'll make it up during the flood time.

Afterwards, Neb and I went to our cave. I should have gone home to help pull leeks up, but we haven't seen each other for ages. I almost wished I hadn't because, after me risking trouble to spend time with him, Neb swore at me! Not *at* me, exactly. I was explaining how to build a reed fence, and drawing a picture in the sand. We put fences like these round a compound, and spread dates out inside, to dry. The fence keeps animals out. And Tiya.

'Stop!' Neb said. 'You're going too fast.

You've got to pick dates before you dry them. How do you pick dates from such tall trees?'

'You climb up.'

'I know,' he said impatiently. 'But how?'

'You just climb,' I said. 'It's easy.'

That's when he swore.

'Easy for you!' he said. 'You've done it all your life. How can I learn how to harvest dates and dry them and make fences if I don't actually *do* it?'

And he left!

Well, fine, I thought. Let him moan. If he got off his bum and made an effort, he could climb a palm. Most kids do it once they're big enough. Or hungry enough. But Neb's family are never hungry.

He could practise on any tree he sees. But what about me? Neb can tell me all about mummy-making, but I can hardly go up to

Simut the fisherman and say, 'Stand still while I mummify you,' can I?

I was scratching out my picture when Neb returned. He flopped down and thumped my arm. His way of saying sorry.

'It's no good us just telling each other,' he said. 'We need experience.'

He's right. And I've got an idea. But I must think about it first.

I've been bent double picking veg for a week, with just one afternoon off. That was only because a goat decided I'd look better with my head against a wall. Father let me stay indoors until I'd finished bleeding.

Father's twitchy. He swears he can see the river rising as he watches.

Most of the fruit's been picked, but we're waiting for some melons to ripen. There are still beans, onions and garlic to harvest, though. We've stored what we can, and swapped what we can't, for things like a bigger bed for my little brother, Baba. A lot of food goes to pay the workers, and Uncle Wadj has a share, too. He pays well for his food.

The men from the government came today, like they do every two years. They measure our fields to make sure Father's not pinching someone else's land by moving the boundary stones.

Which he wouldn't.

They counted our animals and crops to decide how much Father owes in taxes. He came back in a filthy mood. We were all lolling about on the roof stuffing fruit.

'Taxes higher than ever!' he snapped. '*And I'm still expected to work for Pharaoh during the flood,*' he grumbled, flicking a date stone at a passing bird. 'At my age! It's not good leaving a farm idle.' Same moan every year.

'The farm's not idle when it's flooded,' Mother twittered, trying to cheer him up. 'It's being renewed – made richer – so work is being done even when you're away.'

Father rolled his eyes and mouthed, 'Women.'

Tiya joined in. 'You'll upset Hapy if you're grumpy about the flood,' she said.

Hapy's the Nile god, who sees that the flood comes at the same time each year.

'Hoy!' I said, changing the subject. 'Instead of giving the government geese and goats as taxes, let's give them chickens!'

I got such a look, I decided to disappear. As I crossed the yard, Nasty ambushed me from behind. I yelled and kicked at him. He came at me again so I ran. All I could hear were shrieks of laughter – especially from Father!

Later

I don't have to walk so far to the river now – the water's definitely rising and getting wider. I soon spotted Neb on his way back from work. I got in his boat and we paddled to the middle of the river. The current's quite strong now, so we have to keep paddling upstream, to make sure we don't get carried too far north.

'It's akhet season soon,' I said.

'Any fool can see that,' said Neb.

'Akhet's when I don't have to do much on the farm. This is when you can teach me mummy-making.'

Neb paddled furiously upstream. 'But what about me?' he panted. 'When do I learn farming?'

'I'll paddle,' I said. I didn't want to, but I needed time to think of an answer.

'It'd be stupid trying to teach you farming when the whole place is underwater,' I said. 'The best thing is for me to learn all I need to know during akhet, then I can teach you in the peret season! That's when the real farm work happens – when the flood's gone down and we're plough-ing and sowing. You'll love it!'

Neb considered. 'All right,' he said. 'We'll do it. As soon as the flood's high. It won't be so hard for you to get to where I work, either – you can paddle nearly all the way – except you haven't got a boat.'

'No problem,' I said. 'I'm making one! I went to the river this morning and cut some reeds before they were all drowned by the flood.'

People say reed boats are easy to make. They're not.

Father insists the flood's going to be too high this year. He says that every year, but I've checked the Nilometer. The water already is quite high –

up to the tenth step. It had
better not rise much more,
or it'll be bad news for
everybody.

I'll go out most evenings in my boat for a
while. I want Mother and Father to get used to me
disappearing now and then. They'll think I'm
fishing!

Tomorrow I start school again properly.
Father says I can meet up with my friends afterwards if I take some cheese to the woman who
helps Mother with the bees. Great! I'll make
arrangements with Neb to start learning mummy-
making.

School was terrible today. The master droned
on for hours about the pyramids at Giza. I got into
trouble for not listening when I actually was (sort
of) and got a stick across my back. When I got
home I found some bits of used papyrus Uncle
Wadj had given me, and drew the rotten

pyramids on the back. That'll show the master I *was* listening.

First I drew the step pyramid. It's 1400 years old and a bit crumbly now, but it's as tall as 35 men balancing on each other's shoulders.

Next I did the bent pyramid. Somebody messed that one up when they got to the top!

Those pyramids look as if the builders were just practising because the three big ones at Giza are pretty perfect. Khafra's is the big one, with Khufu's middle-sized one and Menkaura's smaller one on either side.

I think my pictures are pretty good. *Now* let the master accuse me of not listening. Who cares, anyway? Something exciting's happening tomorrow! Neb says I can go to where he works! I asked Father, 'If I get up early and work hard before school, can I go fishing in the afternoon?'

'Do your chores and I won't grumble,' he said. I can't wait!

It was very satisfying kicking Nasty out of the chicken house before he was awake this morning. I expect he'll get me back, though.

I took my pictures in, but the master said pyramids was yesterday and I'd better pay attention today or he'd keep me in after school. I wasn't having that, not today of all days, so I listened like I've never listened before! The morning seemed to go on for ever.

After school, Neb went to work. He eats lunch in his boat, bobbing on the water. I went home for some food, got my boat out and paddled across to the west bank.

My first day learning to be a mummy maker! I thought about what it means. Everyone wants to cross over to the Field of Reeds, the afterlife. It's like Egypt there, only better. You have loads of food, and music and fun, and all your friends and family are there (the dead ones). Everyone has a great time. Of course, in order to still have a home for your ka (your life-force) and your ba (your personality), your body needs to be preserved. And that's where the mummy makers come in!

I pulled my boat ashore, and climbed the steep bank. My feet sank in the hot sand, and I slid backwards. Excitement kept me going! I knew that when I reached the top of the rise, I would look down on the Beautiful House for the first time.

Neb was waiting for me just over the top! He sat under a rush canopy stuffing figs.

I went to sit beside him, but he jumped up.

'Come and see where I work,' he said. 'There's no one around at the moment. Be quick. This way.'

He didn't need to show me where to go. I could have found it blindfold. The stink hit me like a rock between the eyes! It was something I'd never expected. For a moment, I wondered what I was letting myself in for. Beautiful House? How could they call it that?

'Fyaw!' I muttered.

Neb grinned. 'Never be a mummy maker if you can't take the smell.'

That fixed me. 'It was just at first,' I said. 'Doesn't bother me now. I can hardly smell it. See?' And I did a huge long sniff.

Whoa! I nearly threw up, there and then, but I was determined not to let Neb see I couldn't take it. I swallowed hard and tried to breathe through my mouth.

Neb showed me the tent where they wash the bodies, and the house where they do the mummy-making, but it was all too much to take in. It's a muddle in my mind now.

I saw a fresh body though. Neb had helped wash it in Nile water, then they shaved all the hair

off. Now it's pure, and ready to be made into a mummy, which Neb says I must call 'embalming'.

I got used to the smell, a bit. If Neb, who hates mummy-making, can stand it, so can I. The Beautiful House does have a special feel to it – to me, at least. It's where bodies are prepared so their owners will live forever. Imagine!

Neb took me into a small room full of old jars, and showed me where he'd gouged a little hole in the wall.

'What's that for?' I asked.

'Put your eye to it,' he said, pleased with himself.

I had a perfect view of the body on the embalming table.

'Whenever you come, just sneak round the back into here, and watch what's going on,' said Neb. 'But if you're caught, you're on your own, right?'

'Right!'

Father's gone to help rebuild part of a
temple wall at Karnak, but I couldn't
get away because I had to watch
Tiya and Baba all day, while
Mother spent hours down at
the   river,   washing
clothes and talking
non-stop to the
other women.

When I went
to the shaduf, to
fetch water for the pigs,
I let Tiya ride the donkey there.

Baba held out his arms
and said, 'Ooo, ooo!' so I
sat him up with Tiya.
When I tried to get him down, he screamed and
hung on to the donkey's mane. I had to drag him
off. He yanked out handfuls of hair and the poor

animal took off with Tiya thumping up and down on his back, screaming, 'Seti, get me!' I dumped Baba and grabbed Tiya before she fell off. By that time, Baba was plastered in donkey droppings. I stood him in a water bucket and washed him.

I wish I was in that smelly mummy-making house.

Free at last today! Mother had her friends round. Whenever their men are away, they spend their spare time in each other's houses talking, eating stuffed dates, and trying each other's cheeses.

I reached the Beautiful House, slipped in the back and into the store room. When I looked through the spy hole I was surprised to see a different body. Two men were laying out tools. My tummy lurched when I realised one of them was Uncle Mose. For a moment I forgot there was a wall between us, and was sure he'd see me. And explode.

I nearly screamed when something touched

58

my back!

'Neb!'

'Keep watching,' he said. 'They're going to take the brain out.'

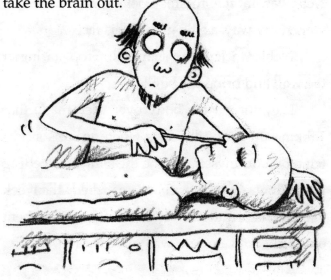

'It's a different body,' I hissed.

'Course it is. You don't think we work on one at a time, do you? It takes seventy days to do a proper job. Half that time the bodies just lie there, drying out. You'll see.'

I turned back to watch. Uncle Mose picked up a long hook thing, and shoved it up the body's nose. Up and up. Where did it go? Even Neb only gets his finger halfway up his nose.

I couldn't see what happened next, because Neb was in the room, blocking my view. He looked my way, a silly grin on his face.

'Neb!' Uncle Mose snapped. 'Stop staring at the wall and bring the bowl.'

They turned the body over. Neb made that yakking-up sound he does when he feels sick. I felt a bit odd myself. Maybe the stink was getting to me. It was worse than our goat sheds the week Father was ill and nobody bothered to clean them out. I checked no one was outside, and slipped away.

On my way to the river, I passed an old man carrying armfuls of linen.

'Who are you, boy?' he asked.

'A friend of Neb's,' I said. 'I came to see if he wanted to play ball.'

'He'll be finished soon,' said the old man. 'I'll tell him you're here.'

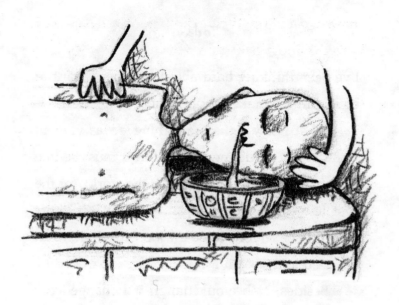

Oops. Not in front of Uncle Mose, I hope!

'You don't look too good,' said the old man. 'Bit pale.'

If I was pale then, I was even paler when Neb told me Uncle Mose pushed the hook up the body's nose into the brain, whooshed it about a bit, then let the brain pour out into the bowl Neb held.

I haven't eaten anything tonight.

Today

I've been thinking hard about whether I want to be a mummy maker or not. And I've decided.

What I saw – the brain thing – was vile, all right, and it made me feel ill. But it must be like that for every mummy maker in the world, for the first few times. If they'd all been put off, there wouldn't be anyone to do the job. No – if they can get used to it, so can I.

Besides, Neb would laugh if I changed my mind.

As I paddled to the west bank, I saw Neb pull his boat up on shore and sit down for a rest. The river's so wide now – almost in full flood – and the current's so strong it's hard work getting across.

When he got up, I yelled, 'Hoy!' and he waited.

'Didn't expect to see you,' he grunted, as we heaved my boat ashore. 'Thought we'd turned your stomach for good.'

I knew it. 'Pish!' I said. 'Can't wait to learn more.' Not strictly true. The brain bit was bad enough.

'You're in luck,' said Neb. 'We're taking someone's organs out today.'

That sounded all right. Except at that point I didn't know what organs are. Now I do.

Neb told me that the embalmer makes a slit in the body's side and takes out the liver, lungs, stomach and intestines. They get mummified separately. The heart, which holds your memory, stays in. Neb said the brain's chucked away because it's useless. It doesn't do anything, so it's not important in the afterlife.

This was gruesome, but not

as bad as the brain business. Maybe I'm getting used to it already.

I forgot to wash on the way home. Mother took one look at me – or rather had one sniff – and told me to get in the animals' water trough and clean myself up.

Then she said that as I'd been out playing all afternoon, I could help her. I had to grind grain.

I put wheat grains on a stone, then ground them to flour with another stone – for hours . . . and hours . . .

Now I feel worn out but I'm going back to Neb's tomorrow.

Today I met Neb in the village while I was getting new sandals. I paid with a cold roast goose, a small basket of pomegranates and a chick, which the sandal maker wasn't excited about.

'Foreign rubbish!' he snorted.

'You'll love it,' I lied. 'They're no trouble.'

My new sandals are made of papyrus. It's fantastic stuff, papyrus. You can write on it, walk on it, make boats out of it – even ropes.

My old leather sandals fell to bits. Father says I'm growing too fast. The real problem is I'm treading in water so much these days that my sandals simply rotted. The fields are completely flooded now, and I'm either launching my boat from oozy mud, or rescuing stupid goats that have tumbled into ditches. Not chickens, though. If chickens fall in a ditch, that's their problem.

Father can't understand me and chickens. I show him the stab marks on my ankles, but he laughs and says, 'Ant bites!' Some ants!

I have to take a broom when I go to the toilet. I wish the entrance to ours was indoors, but Mother says it's revolting and should stay outside. When the pot's full, we empty it into a hole in the ground, because it's good for the soil. I'm tempted to empty it over Nasty!

Neb's promised me a surprise when I go to the embalming house. 'But you must come today,' he said. 'Late afternoon? When it's empty? I'll wait for you.'

I worked so fast, even during the hottest part of the day when everyone else was resting, that Mother said I could go fishing later. 'As you spend so much time with your net, perhaps you'll catch something we can all enjoy for dinner.'

Oops.

Before I left, I sneaked two goose eggs from the kitchen.

The river's so wide that Neb was just a speck on the far bank as I paddled across. Everywhere's so different. It's hard to believe that in a few weeks the water will be gone and we'll be planting rotten seeds again.

As we climbed the bank I wondered about the surprise – was it something for our cave? A lamp, so we could go there at night? Or a new fishing net? Mine's full of holes. I know there are supposed to be holes, but a baby hippo could get its head through these. And you don't want to snare a baby hippo!

We went into the empty embalming house.

'Close your eyes,' said Neb.

He flung something down on the table. Thud!

'Look.'

I opened my eyes. I couldn't believe what I was seeing.

A dead rat.

'It's fresh,' said Neb. 'It's for you to make your first mummy. Come on, let's get started.'

I was speechless.

'Well? Do you or don't you want to be an embalmer?' Neb demanded.

His question startled me. It's exactly what I do want, and the rat is my first step on that path.

We didn't bother washing it in the Nile. Neb had a pail of water that did the same job. Next I shaved my rat, which was difficult. Neb didn't make it any easier, bawling instructions: 'Down a bit . . . no, over . . . steady, you'll have its ear off.' When I'd finished, it looked a bit like the stubbly coconut Uncle Wadj brought back from a seaport in the north.

I wasn't sure about removing the brain. 'It's probably too small to find,' I said, hoping Neb would agree. 'I expect the rat sneezed it out long ago.'

We decided not to bother with the brain, but Neb said I must get the organs out. 'They should be washed and bandaged,' he said, 'but you needn't do that for a rat.'

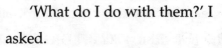

'What do I do with them?' I
asked.

'You ought to put them in
canopic jars,' he said. 'We haven't
got any to spare, but I found these. They're
cracked.' He gave me four small jugs and said I
could make stoppers out of mud.

'Here.' Neb handed me a knife.

I took a deep breath. If I didn't do
this, I'd never be a mummy maker.

Oh, yuk and *ugh* and EEUCK! I made

such a mess. I don't know what I got out, but at least I did it. I did it, *I did it*, I DID IT!

'What next?' I asked. I felt so proud of myself, I was ready for anything.

We went into a side room. There was a body shape in a sort of trough, covered with something like sand, only paler.

'After the body's been cleaned inside and out,' said Neb, 'it has to have all the fluid taken out, otherwise it will rot. Natron salt does the job. This man will be covered in it for forty days.'

'I don't have to leave the rat for forty days, do I?' I asked. 'The flood will be falling back by then. I'll be working all the time.'

'*And* teaching me how to farm,' said Neb. 'You haven't forgotten, have you, Seti?'

'No, no!' I said quickly. (I had, just about.)

We decided that as a rat's so small, twenty days would probably be enough.

Neb gave me a wooden box. 'I made it,' he said. 'For me?'

'For the rat, stupid. Cover it with natron salt, and we'll hide it.'

We put the rat-in-a-box behind a stack of cracked urns that Neb said were no use, so nobody would disturb them.

What will I find in two weeks' time? And what will I learn in the meantime?

On the way home, Simut the fisherman was bringing in his nets. I got the goose eggs from my boat and swapped them for a nice fat carp.

'You'll eat like a king tonight,' said Simut, laughing at me struggling to keep hold of the slippery fish.

He's wrong of course. Kings never eat fish. But we do! And Mother *was* impressed. Until she saw the state of my hands.

'Go and wash,' she said, 'and not in my nice clean water! Go to the river, and take Tiya with you. She's been under my feet all day.'

We set off.

'I saw you talking to Simut the fisherman,' said Tiya.

Pish! Did she see me swap the eggs for the fish?

'What were you talking about, Seti?' she asked.

'Er, Osiris,' I said. 'He told me the story of Osiris and the fish.'

She tucked her hand in mine and smiled at me sweetly. 'Tell me,' she commanded.

We'd reached the edge of the river. She sat,

and pulled me down beside her. Perhaps, I thought, if I tell her the tale of Osiris, she'll forget about seeing me with Simut.

'All right,' I said, 'but I must be quick, because it's nearly time to eat.' I lay back and she lay down, too, with her chin in her hands and her elbows digging in my tummy.

'Osiris,' I began, 'was once the ruler of Egypt. He had a lovely wife called –'

'Isis,' said Tiya. 'I know.'

'Osiris had a brother called Seth, who was very jealous of him,' I went on. 'He made a coffin that would only fit one person.'

Tiya nodded. 'Osiris.'

'That's right,' I said. 'And he told Osiris that whoever the coffin fitted, could have it. So Osiris said, "I'll try it," and got in.'

'And Seth slammed the lid on the coffin and said, "Good riddance!" and threw it in the Nile.'

I tickled Tiya's nose.

'Who's telling this story?'

'You. Go on.'

'Isis wanted her husband back, and she searched far and wide until she found his coffin.'

'Now the nasty bit,' said Tiya.

'Seth chopped Osiris's body into fourteen pieces and buried each bit in a different place along the river.

each bit in a different place along the river.

'Did Isis give up?' asked Tiya.

'Not her! She hunted down the body parts, and the jackal-headed god –'

'Anubis.'

'Yes, Anubis,' I agreed. 'He helped her put Osiris back together, and bandaged him to hold the bits together.'

'His first mummy!'

'And then,' I said, 'Isis used her powers to

bring Osiris to life, long enough for them to have
a baby.'

'Horus, the falcon god.'

I stood up and pulled Tiya to
her feet. 'Isis hid Horus among
the Nile reeds until he was old
enough to fight his father's
murderer.'

'Seth.'

'There was a great fight,' I
said, leading her back towards
home. 'Horus lost an eye, but

he killed Seth and became the King of Egypt. Osiris became king of the dead.'

'And, Tiya, because some of Osiris's body bits had been nibbled by fish, from that day to this, kings have never, ever had fish for dinner.'

'Then I'm glad I'm not a king,' said greedy Tiya. She squeezed my hand. 'That was a lovely story, Seti. I've never heard it before.'

What a little liar.

She skipped off up the hill. 'And as you've been so nice to me,' she called over her shoulder, 'I won't tell Mother about the eggs!'

⟦ʊꕄꙮꕔ⟧

I wake each morning bursting to go to the Beautiful House. Today I helped Mother as much as possible, hoping she'd give me time off. I even offered to feed the chickens.

'Oh, please feed them!' said wicked Tiya. 'I love watching you feed them!'

'You love watching Nasty trying to eat my ankles,' I said. 'Take the broom and sweep him away from me. He never bothers you.'

I ran to the chicken house, strewing food as I went, and hoping Nasty might be hungry enough to eat first and chase later. No such luck. As he attacked, Tiya collapsed with laughter.

'Broom him! Thump him!' I cried, dancing across the yard like a baboon on hot sand. Everyone laughed: Mother, Tiya, the workers – even Baba shook his little fists, crying, 'Woo, woo!'

At least I had the afternoon free. Neb had to collect some statuettes from the craftsmen's village. I went with him.

Neb took two donkeys – one for himself, and one to carry the statuettes back – so we both rode to the craftsmen's village.

There must be over sixty houses, all sheltered by cliffs. Many of the best craftsmen live there. They're well paid, and their food and water is brought to them, because the village is in the desert. Must be nice, fiddling about with paint and having everything delivered!

Neb loaded the statuettes on the spare donkey, while I held the other one, which kept nibbling my kilt. I was scared it was going to rip it off – I wasn't wearing a loincloth!

On the way back, I asked Neb what the statuettes were for.

'They're shabti,' he said. 'People want them buried in their tombs. When you reach the afterlife, you need servants to grow food and do the work. That's what shabti are for. They're little servants.'

I could do with a shabti in our chicken house.

Father's back from Karnak, and I've barely had a minute to myself ever since. He's kept me so busy I can only *dream* about going to see Neb.

We've got too many onions in our store, so this afternoon we loaded some into Father's boat, and went down river to the village. Tiya came, too. Father was happy sitting with her under a canopy, trading the onions and catching up on the news. He let me wander off. I headed straight for Neb's street and hung about. A girl shouted, 'Hoy! You looking for Neb?'

'Yeah.'

'He went up there.' The girl pointed in the direction of our cave. 'He's done that a lot these past few days.'

I tore uphill and, sure enough, Neb was in the cave, drawing an ostrich in the sand with his toe. He looked glad to see me.

'We've got a body coming out of natron in five days' time,' he said. 'You ought to see it before they start bandaging.'

'Five days – I'll be there!' I glanced outside. The sun was low. 'I'd better get back. Father will be wondering where I am.'

I got up, but Neb pulled me back down.

'What?' I said.

He dug up our treasure box, blew the sand off, opened it and took out the two scarabs. 'Here.'

'*What*?' I said again.

'Remember our pact? Let's swear again.'

I was mystified. 'Why? I haven't forgotten it.'

'Because,' said Neb, 'all the teaching's being done by me. I haven't learned a thing about farming, except that you can swap four eggs for a fish and impress your mother.'

'It's not my fault,' I said. 'The water will soon go down, and we'll be planting and sowing for weeks. You'll learn about it right from the beginning – that's best.'

He nodded. 'Suppose so.'

'Here.' I put both scarabs in his hand, then pressed my open hand on top. 'Pact?'

'Pact.'

We galloped downhill and were almost at the market when I heard Tiya's voice. 'Seti!'

'Pish!' Neb and I froze in horror. He ducked smartly down behind a passing string of donkeys. Father came towards us. Had he seen?

He hadn't. Good thing he didn't bother to count the legs of the donkeys trotting past!

Five more days and I'll learn the next stage of mummy-making.

Father's taking us to Karnak to make offerings at the temple. I love going there, but why now? He's dithering about whether to go tomorrow or the next day. The next day's when the body's coming out of natron!

'Tomorrow!' I said.

'I don't know,' he muttered. 'The chicken house needs cleaning. If I don't do it soon, I'll get behind . . . I believe the flood's going down . . . better do it tomorrow . . . we'll go the day after.'

'Tomorrow, please,' I begged. 'I'll clean the chicken house!'

Mother smiled. 'I must say, I'm looking forward to a day out.'

'Me, too!' said Tiya.

Baba said, 'Too, too!'

'I promise I'll do the chicken house,' I said, making my eyes go big like Tiya does when she wants something.

Father laughed. 'Properly, mind, or I'll tip you upside down and sweep it out with your hair!'

We're going tomorrow!

Next day

We took so much stuff to Karnak, it's a wonder our boat didn't sink. Mother always over-does her picnics!

She carried Baba, and the rest of us took the fruit and veg we're offering to Amun, the mighti-est of all the gods. We left our picnic in the boat, covered with reeds to keep the sun off, and made our way to the front of the temple. I stood at the end of the avenue of the ram-headed sphinxes, which is so long Father said it would take him an hour to walk it! There must be hundreds of sphinxes along the way.

First Father showed us where he'd helped mend the outside wall. When it was first built, someone left it with a flat top when they finished

for the night. The top of the wall's supposed to be wavy, and when a priest saw it was flat, he went mad and bashed it down. It had to be rebuilt.

Once inside the wall, I couldn't take my eyes off the massive pylon. It's a great gateway, made up of two towers, with the entrance between.

Priests in gleaming white robes were everywhere. Father said there are thousands of them at Karnak alone. I didn't believe him, but a man nearby said it's true.

'They don't just look after the temple,' he said.

'There are schools, animals, fields, workshops . . .' He pointed to the pylon. 'Did you know there's a doctor's room inside there?'

I did, because Father told me, but I pretended I didn't, and he gave me a honey-dipped pastry. I shared it with Baba and Tiya, and then we had our picnic. Good thing we were going down-stream when we went home – my tummy was so full I could hardly paddle.

I was as fidgety as a frog this morning. Father checked the fields, seeing how far down the water's gone (not far enough). I had loads of small jobs to do. I rushed through them, grabbed my fishing net and tore off.

'Set – eeee!' came Mother's voice. I kept going.

'Seti!' she screeched. 'You forgot . . .' I couldn't hear any more.

Neb saw me coming. When I reached the far bank, he said, 'They haven't left yet. Hide!'

Hide? Where? The flood's covered just about everything. In the end I bobbed about on the water with my head down, pretending to be fishing. As soon as I saw the embalmers get into their boats and push off, I paddled ashore.

Neb dragged me to the Beautiful House. 'Look at this!' he said. 'It's spectacular!'

Spectacular? Hardly! The body on the table looked like someone who hadn't eaten for months. And it was dark brown!

'It's small,' I said.

'They all go like that,' said Neb. 'Wait till you see your rat. Only six days to go.'

I asked Neb what happens next to this thin, dark body.

'I'll show you,' he said. We went through an arch. There was another thin, dark body there, and it actually smelled quite nice.

'It's fatter than the other one,' I said.

'That's because after we wash the natron off, we stuff all the empty bits, where the stomach and stuff were. It makes it look more normal.'

'What do you stuff it with?'

'Sawdust, and linen soaked in resin,' said Neb. 'That stops it rotting on the inside. And before you ask,' he said, as I opened my mouth, 'resin comes from pine trees. They grow a long way away.'

'What smells nice?' I asked.

'The body's been rubbed with scented oils,' said Neb. 'It feels horrible doing that – all knobbly. Come on, I'd better get home.'

We went back through the stinky room. Now I'm over the gruesome bit, I know this is what I really want to do. The embalmers will make sure that person lives forever. What's a bit of a stink compared to that?

I left the stink behind and washed in the river before I went home (without a fish).

Father greeted me. Well, I say greeted. What he actually did was take me by the ear and march me straight to the chicken house. I'd completely forgotten my promise.

'Clean it before you get a single mouthful of food,' he said.

What with him pinching my ear, and Nasty pecking my shins, I couldn't have felt more miserable.

I got my broom and poo scraper, took a deep breath, went into the chicken house and shut the door, leaving Nasty outside.

Anyone who can stand the smell of embalming, I thought, can stand an hour or so in a chicken house. I scraped and scrubbed, scraped and scrubbed, till suddenly the door opened and

Tiya's hand waved a piece of bread at me.

I was just about to take it when, with a furious squawking, in burst Nasty, feathers flying and wings flapping. He went straight for my feet, so I leaped over him, fell outside, and slammed the door shut. Nasty was trapped.

I ate my bread. Even Tiya was disgusted at the state of my hands. Of course, once I wanted to get going again, Nasty wouldn't come out, so I had to clean round him. He squatted, glaring at me with his horrible eyes like glittering beads.

Every time I moved near, he attacked me. Now we have a lovely clean chicken house, all except for one filthy corner, which I hope I won't have to explain to Father.

Rat day!

I couldn't wait to take my rat out of natron. What would it look like? I hurried through my chores and at last the time

came. I ran down to the river, clutching my net, so everyone would think I was fishing. As I threw it into the boat, I heard a small voice behind me. Tiya!

'I want to go fishing,' she said.

Oh no! I threatened her with angry hippos, crocodiles, water snakes, even a giant heron that feeds its babies with small girls. All she said was, 'I want to go fishing.'

In the end, I promised that if she went home, I'd bring her back a present.

'All right.'

I pushed the boat off and jumped in.

Tiya cupped her hands round her mouth. 'Don't forget my present!' she called. 'Or I'll tell!' She ran back uphill.

Tell? What did she mean? Tell what?

I forgot about Tiya when a long wooden boat containing Uncle Mose headed towards me. I changed direction and paddled in among a group of boys and girls who were messing about, trying

to push each other in the water. I jumped in with them, splashed about a bit and waited for the wooden boat to go past.

As soon as Uncle Mose had gone, I made for the west bank. Soon I'd be taking my rat out of natron. How long before I'll be helping an embalmer somewhere to take out a human body? I know I can't work in Neb's embalming house as long as Uncle Mose is alive. But there are plenty more.

Neb had promised to get the rat-in-a-box out ready for me, but I couldn't see it. 'Where's my rat?' I asked.

'Still in the box,' he said.

'Let's see.'

Neb shook his head. 'Trust me, you don't want to do that,' he said. 'It hasn't been in natron long enough. Leave it another week.'

'Another week!' I said. 'Neb, the flood's going down. Soon it'll be peret season and I'll be so busy with the farm and school I won't be able to get here for months!'

Neb told me something I could do in the meantime. 'Start collecting linen for the bandaging.'

'Don't the embalmers supply it?' I asked.

He laughed. 'It's too expensive!' he said. 'Do you know, some people collect linen all their lives, just so they can be buried in it? They either make it, or earn it, or swap goods for it.'

I realised how often Mother sits weaving linen. We hardly ever have new clothes, so she must be putting it away somewhere. But where?

As I paddled home, I decided to see if I could find Mother's linen, but Tiya was at my throat as soon as I got home. I'd forgotten her present.

'I'll tell about you going across the river,' she said. 'I'll tell Father you meet a boy over there. You do! I've seen you.'

Gods alive! That would mean a few awkward questions! I swore to remember next time, as long as she keeps quiet.

Later

I feel bad.

I discovered where Mother keeps her linen. There's loads of it, so I helped myself to a length. I won't need much for my rat.

I was about to tear it into strips when I thought, What am I doing! This linen's been carefully made and hoarded so it'll be there, ready, when my parents die. It's to wrap their bodies in preparation for their journey to the afterlife. And I was about to rip it up for a *rat*! What's the matter with me?

When I go to Neb's, I'll tell him I haven't got any linen yet. The afterlife can wait a little longer for my rat.

𓂀𓏤𓆓𓏏

The flood's definitely gone down over the last couple of days. The river has a border of rich black silt. The farmers are out each day, sniffing it and predicting what a good year it's going to be.

Tiya watched me go to the river. She said nothing, just watched until I was out of sight. I got a sharp stone and scraped the back of my hand. A line of white appeared, then it turned red. That would remind me about her present. What it would be, I hadn't a clue.

Neb was washing tools in the river when I arrived.

'Ready?' I asked, excitedly.

'What for?' he said, teasing me.

At the embalming house, he put the tools away. We went into the store room and got out my rat-in-a-box.

I thought there'd be some sort of ceremony, but Neb just put his hand over the top of the box, tipped it upside down, caught the rat and let the natron drop through his spread fingers.

The rat had certainly shrunk. It smelled disgusting, and there were still bits of stubble all over it.

'Now what?' I asked.

Behind me, a deep voice said, 'That's exactly what I'd like to know.'

Neb's face went pale. Slowly, I turned.

Uncle Mose!

He stared at me in disbelief. 'Seti? Seti!'

Neb looked so terrified that I tried to keep him out of it.

'I – I've got this rat . . . I wanted to embalm it . . . I didn't know who to ask . . . I came over here . . . I was so surprised to see Neb –'

'Enough!' Uncle Mose put his hands up. 'Seti, stop shaking, come outside and tell me the truth.'

We sat in the shade, all three of us, and shared some beer. I told Uncle Mose how I longed to be a mummy maker, and how I had to be a farmer, which I hate. I didn't mention the pact. I could see Neb was terrified I might – he could hardly swallow his beer.

I gabbled about how difficult it is to learn mummy-making. 'I have to come in secret, pretending to be fishing.' I held up my scratched hand. 'And I've promised Tiya a present to shut her up. I've got just so far with my rat, but I don't have oils or resin . . . as for linen for bandages, well it's hopeless . . . I might as well give up and breed chickens . . .'

'Chickens?' said Uncle Mose.

'They're horrible,' I said.

He listened and listened. He isn't a monster. In the end, all he said was, 'Come to our house tomorrow, Seti –'

'I can't!' I blurted out. 'Father would murder me.'

Uncle Mose looked thoughtful. Then he smiled. 'In that case, come back to the embalming house as soon as you can. We'll talk again.' He stood up. 'Now let's wash, otherwise we'll all be in trouble when we go home.'

Before we left, Neb slipped back into the embalming house and came out with something stuffed down his kilt.

As I climbed into my boat, Neb reached into the top of his kilt and pressed something into my hand.

'For Tiya,' he said. 'To keep her quiet.'

I wondered just how long that would be necessary.

Next day

Last night I felt that the words
'Uncle Mose' were carved on
my forehead.

I couldn't settle all
evening. It was boiling.
Everyone slept on the roof,
but I wanted to be alone, so I
went downstairs, flung the door
wide and sweltered. I woke up with two ducks
snuggled into me.

I couldn't even eat breakfast. Mother eyed
me suspiciously. 'Are you ill, Seti?'

I said no, but I was nearly sick when Father
picked up the present I'd given Tiya.

'A shabti?' he said. 'What's a shabti doing
here?'

Tiya held out her hands. 'It's mine.' She took
it, and looked directly at me. 'I found it. Didn't I,
Seti?'

Father was puzzled. 'It's not the sort of thing that's usually left lying around,' he said. 'Seti, what –?'

He was interrupted by Nasty strutting through the doorway. One thing Father won't have is animals in the house, so I knew it was safe to get the broom and shoosh Nasty out. I swept him, squawking and complaining, right across the yard.

That's the first time the ugly bird's ever done me a favour. I hugged Tiya and went to check the donkeys.

Today, Father had to mend a fence on the far side of the farm. I took a chance, slipped away and crossed the river.

It seemed strange walking into the embalming house while it was busy and alive. Uncle Mose waved. His hand was sticky with something – I didn't like to think what.

'Take this,' he said, handing me a metal pot.

'Neb's going to melt it. Watch what he does.'

Neb was melting resin for brushing on a body. It stops the mummy rotting and stinking apparently.

When the resin had melted, Neb gave it to an assistant, and Uncle Mose took us outside.

'Seti, I've been thinking,' he said. 'Pepy – your father – and I will never see eye to eye –'

'Why not?' Neb asked.

Uncle Mose glared. 'I've told you,' he said sharply, 'I'm not discussing it!' He turned to me.

'Seti, are you serious about becoming an embalmer?'

I felt a fool, because my eyes were teary and all I could do was nod. I longed to say it's what I want most of all, but I couldn't speak.

He smiled. 'You may learn alongside Neb. As far as the other workers here are concerned, I am treating my nephew as my son. But,' he went on, 'your father mustn't know. How you get here, and how you find the time is up to you.' He smiled. 'You've managed to deceive everyone so far. I'm sure it will be no problem.'

'It won't,' I said. 'Thank you, Uncle Mose.'

'What about when Seti's grown up?' asked Neb crossly. 'What will he do then? Be a farmer or an embalmer?'

Uncle Mose shrugged. 'Time takes care of many things.'

〔ᴎ〕〔≙〕〔◉〕〔¬〕

It's been almost a month since Uncle Mose started teaching me. I'm totally worn out. The flood's just about cleared our fields, and I've worked non-stop. Every time Father said, 'Go and amuse yourself for a while, Seti – you've done well,' I've hurried to get to the Beautiful House before the embalmers finish for the day. There's been no time for school, but I've been learning more important things!

The dead person wants to look good in the afterlife, so once the body's been sealed, someone makes up the face. Then his best wig is fitted.

Next, a plate's put over the cut where they took out the innards. It has a wedjat eye on it. It stops anything bad, like evil spells, getting in through the cut.

There's so much to learn.

104

After this comes the bandaging. Uncle Mose promised I'll see that soon, but it can't be difficult.

When Neb and I paddled back to the east bank today, he said, 'Let's go to the cave, Seti. We haven't been there for ages.'

'I can't,' I said. 'I think I saw Tiya coming to look for me.'

That wasn't true, but I knew what Neb wanted, and I didn't want to talk about it.

〔𓄿𓏤𓊖𓏤〕

In the morning I had to go to the doctor's to get some medicine. Baba keeps coughing.

'If the doctor's out visiting patients,' said Father, 'you might have to wait. Could you amuse yourself for an hour or so?'

'Of course, Father,' I said.

Yes! A couple of hours was just what I needed. I planned to go straight to the doctor's, then across the river to watch some bandaging. Then home again, pretending I'd waited hours for the doctor. But have I been in trouble!

I went to the doctor's and asked for medicine for Baba.

'What sort of a cough is it?' the doctor asked.

'Haaargh! Haaargh!'

The doctor closed his eyes briefly. 'I didn't ask for a demonstration. Is it a dry cough or a chesty cough?'

Well, *I* didn't know.

'I really should see Baba,' he said, 'but I'll give you something for him. Let's see . . . honey . . . spices . . .'

He mumbled on as he mixed the medicine. I took it and ran.

He shouted after me, 'I really ought . . .' But I pretended not to hear.

At the embalming house, they were bandaging two bodies at once. It smelled funny in there. Not rotting-body funny, but scented and smoky. Uncle Mose said a special priest, called a lector, comes in before the bandaging and wafts incense around, to purify the air.

Bandaging's complicated and it takes 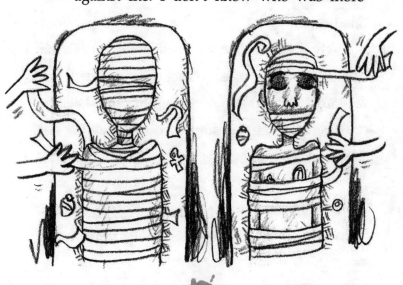 days to complete. While you're doing it, you slip special little amulets in among the layers of bandage.

Uncle Mose said a scarab is often laid over the heart, or hung round the mummy's neck. It made me think of my scarab. Is that where it will end up? Over my dead body?

The last thing put on the mummy is a mask, but I couldn't wait for that. I made my way home, only to find the gods had turned against me. I don't know who was more aggressive when I got back – Nasty or Father.

'Where've you been?' Father demanded as I danced away from Nasty. 'And leave my cockerel alone!'

'It pecks me!' I protested.

'I'll do more than peck you if you don't tell me the truth.'

It turned out that the doctor had decided to combine collecting his fee with a look at Baba, so Father found out I'd gone there first thing, and wanted to know where I'd been ever since.

Baba was still waiting, coughing, for his medicine.

They weren't convinced that I'd got talking to friends and stopped to shoot a few arrows. For a start, I didn't have my bow with me. Luckily, they're going out to dinner, so they haven't got time to keep questioning me.

They've gone, and Tiya and Baba are asleep. Time to myself at last! Mother and Father fiddled for ages with their make-up and wigs. Mother did look lovely.

Father used black kohl on his eyes, but Mother wore the lot – kohl, green eye liner, red cheeks and lips painted with powder mixed with oil. They're wearing real hair wigs, not wool ones, and I know what state

they'll be in when they come home – all greasy with scented fat from the incense cones the host will give them to put on their heads while they eat. Yuk! Imagine it!

'I want to play senet,' said Tiya, when they'd gone. 'You want to play, too,' she said, looking me in the eye. 'Don't you?'

I knew if I didn't, she'd tell about me going across the river. So out came the senet board.

I let Tiya win every time, but she wanted to play on and on.

All the time, Baba was coughing, 'Hoo, hoo!' I felt bad. If I'd brought his medicine sooner, he'd be better by now.

Today Father and I took three kid goats to market. I'd just tied them up when I spotted Neb peering round a corner. He beckoned to me.

When I went over, Neb dragged me round the corner. 'The farmers are talking about ploughing next week,' he said. 'You'll be ploughing, won't you?'

'We've started already.' I knew what was coming.

'You promised, Seti,' he said. 'We made a pact. If I taught you mummy-making, you'd teach me farming. Well, the time's come.'

'It's difficult.' I tried to explain. 'You can't hide someone on a farm. Father's always around. He doesn't go home after work like Uncle Mose. He lives where he works.'

Neb's face went hard. He stalked away.

I must have looked worried because when I went back to Father, he said, 'Problem, Seti?'

Just then, a woman asked about the kid goats. Father knows her – she's married to a bead maker. They quickly made an arrangement about a matching hair ornament and girdle for Mother, and the woman took the kids.

'Father,' I said, as we drank our beer. 'I've got a friend who'd like to come and see how we plough and plant and everything. He's really interested. Is it all right if he wanders round now and then?'

'One of your school friends?' said Father.

'Yes.'

'Fine. Just don't let him take you away from your own work.'

'I won't,' I said. My heart felt lighter. It was beating fast, too – probably because I was sort of lying. 'I'll go and tell him.'

But I couldn't find Neb.

It's two days since I've seen Neb, so as soon as I got away this afternoon, I crossed the river and hurried to the embalming house.

Uncle Mose was surprised to see me. 'Neb said you won't be coming any more,' he said.

'I want to, but we're too busy on the farm,' I

explained. 'Can I talk to Neb?'

'He's at the dentist's,' said Uncle Mose. 'He's got toothache.'

Our dentist's father was the dentist before him, and when he pulled some of his son's teeth out (agony!) he put gold ones in their place! I hope that doesn't happen to Neb!

'When Neb's better, will you get him to meet me?' I asked. 'He knows where. I'll go there each day at the time he normally finishes work.'

I went to the cave three days running. No Neb. Then today, I was in there, killing time by scratching a picture for Tiya on an ostracon I pinched from school, when I heard him coming.

'Got your message,' he said.

'How's the tooth?' I asked.

'Gone,' he said.

'Did it hurt much?'

'Torture,' he said.

I held out the scarabs. 'It's all arranged, Neb. Father says you can come to the farm and learn farming.'

'Yeah?' His face lit up. 'But how? What made him say yes? Will our families be friends now? Oh! I daren't tell Father I'm learning farming – he'll think I don't want to work with him.'

'Well, you don't!' I said. 'Anyway, you can't tell, because my father thinks it's a school friend who wants to come – not my cousin.'

'You're stupid, Seti,' he said. 'He's probably seen me . . . He'll recognise me.'

'I'm not stupid,' I said. 'Just stay away from him. The farm's a big place. When he's sowing seeds, I'll show you how we raise water. When he's feeding the sheep, I'll show you ploughing.'

We put the scarabs back and buried the box.

A week later

Apart from me not having time to visit the Beautiful House, things are working out well. Neb's had a go with the hoe, knocking out weeds, and he's tried the plough.

Although oxen pull the plough, it's still hard work – gives you blisters!

We sowed a field today, and Father left me to send in the sheep, so I let Neb help.

The sheep tread in the seeds to save us raking soil over them. Also, birds can't get at them and the wind won't blow them away.

Neb's not bad at handling animals.

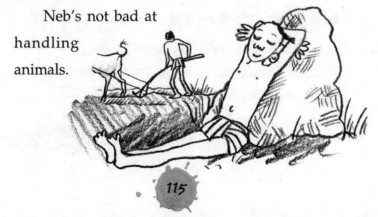

Next day

Disaster! All my fault. One of our workers, who thinks Neb's a school friend, said, 'That boy's a natural! He can do anything with animals. Not like you, eh?'

I was jealous, I suppose. I wanted to make Neb look a fool. So while Mother was out, I made him feed the chickens. He took a scoop of food and I said, 'Walk towards them and chuck it around.'

I felt really smug when Nasty picked up speed and charged. Only he didn't stop! Nasty, I mean! He sped straight past Neb! I yelled but that vicious bird is fast! Before I could run, he was pecking my ankles, stabbing me with his sharp beak until I stumbled and sat down. Splat!

Goat pee.

Neb collapsed with laughter. I glared at him, but he suddenly looked past me, and his face froze. I turned.

It was Father.

'Hello,' he said. 'Is this the friend who wants to . . .' He peered at Neb. 'Don't I know you?'

Neb was too frightened to answer.

There was a moment's hush, then Father turned to me, his voice dangerously quiet. 'What in the name of the great god Amun do you think you're playing at?'

'Uncle Pepy . . .' Neb began, but Father was having none of it.

'Has my brother sent you to spy on me? See how my farm's doing? I built this place up myself! Mose needn't think he's getting his hands on this, as well.'

As well? I didn't understand. Just then, Mother appeared with the little ones. Tiya ran to hug me. Baba sat on the floor copying Father's cross noises.

'Calm down, Pepy,' said Mother. 'Whatever's the . . .' She stopped. 'Neb? It's Neb!'

Father nearly exploded. 'I'm not stupid, woman! I know it's Neb!'

The shouting seemed to go on for ages. In the end, Neb got so upset he just spun round and ran.

'You can run!' yelled Father. 'But you won't get away with this. I'm coming to see your father tomorrow.'

I wanted to explain, but I couldn't just say, 'I don't want this farm when I'm grown up. I want to be a mummy maker.' Anyway, he wouldn't let me explain. I practically got thrown up on to the roof.

As if I can sleep!

Later

I'm still here. I'm scared to go downstairs. All I can hear are cross voices. Tiya's beside me, going on about people coming up the hill. I don't care who comes up the hill. It won't be Neb, will it?

Even Later

It *was* Neb! And Uncle Mose!

When Father came face to face with his brother, it was like two mad bulls glaring into each other's eyes.

Uncle Mose spoke first. 'Neb told me what he's up to.'

'Spying,' growled Father.

'Spying, pah! Neb simply wanted to learn how to farm. That's no worse than what *your* son's been up to.'

Father's jaw snapped shut. He turned to me. 'What have you been up to?'

I swallowed. 'I've been going to the embalming house.'

'Why?'

'To learn how to make mummies.'

'What? *Why*?'

I saw Neb shake his head slightly. 'Just interested,' I mumbled. 'Like Neb's interested in farming.'

They're not stupid, Father and Uncle Mose. They soon wormed out the truth – that I want to be a mummy maker and Neb wants to be a farmer.

'You can forget that!' Father told me.

'You, too!' Uncle Mose said to Neb.

So, that's it. I'm never to speak to Neb again. I'm leaving school immediately. I must stay on the farm for two whole weeks. I'll never be a mummy maker. Father says I've got to learn to love the farm. And the rotten chickens. From now on, I'm in charge of them. The chicken house must be kept spotless, and if I lose so much as one baby chick . . .

A week later

Another long, dreary day. This evening Father told me to stop moping and make myself useful instead.

'Start teaching Tiya her numbers,' he said.

'Yes, Father,' I said, thinking that if I'm co-operative he might let me off with a week of being trapped here instead of two. 'Come along, Tiya.'

Tiya likes the figure with upraised arms best. It's the one for when there are more things than

you can count, like stars in the sky. I was only doing this to sweeten Father, but I actually like teaching Tiya. She has a clever heart.

Father was pleased with me, so while he was in a good mood I thought, Pish! I'll ask him why he hates Uncle Mose.

'Theft!' he growled. 'Mose stole something precious from me.'

Later I asked Mother what Mose had stolen.

'Oh, don't you start!' she said. 'Ridiculous, the whole thing!'

Two weeks of solid hard work! Today's the last day and I've spent it scaring birds off the seedlings. Tomorrow Father's giving me two hours off. That's not as generous as it seems. The days are quite short now, so each of the twelve hours is short, too.

I spent my whole two hours in the cave that day, hoping Neb would come. I've waited each day since. Today I was about to dig up our box, half hoping the scarabs might work some magic and make him come, but before I could, he turned up.

'Hello,' he said. 'Come to collect your things?'

'No!' I said. 'I've been here nearly every day, hoping you'd come. Why? Have you come to take your things?'

He hesitated. 'No.'

Liar.

Neb said his father was really upset. 'He can't believe I don't want to be a mummy maker.'

'The worst thing is we can't be friends,' I said.

'I know,' said Neb. 'Just because they've fallen out, I don't see why we have to suffer.'

He'd discovered why they'd quarrelled so long ago. 'Your father stole something precious from my father,' he said.

I was just about to thump him when I realised that's exactly what my father said about Uncle Mose.

'See if you can find out any more,' I said. 'Ask your mother, and let's meet tomorrow.'

'It's school,' said Neb.

'I've got to take our spare chicks to market,' I said. 'We'll meet afterwards.'

I managed to sell the chicks. The leatherworker's wife took six! In exchange, her husband will mend our oxen's harness.

'These chicks grow up right tasty,' she said.

'Tell your friends!' I begged. 'I want to get rid

of as many as I can.' I'd like to get rid of them all. Especially Nasty.

Neb arrived wrapped in a winter cloak.

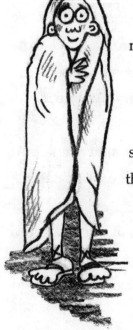

'You'll cook in that,' I said.

'I don't want anyone to see me,' Neb explained.

'Did you talk to your mother?'

Neb nodded. 'She says she's sick of the whole stupid thing and won't discuss it.'

Neb and I talked and talked, and we've decided it's mad for families not to be friends. We're going to fix things so they meet in public, where they can't start shouting.

Today was the day!

I told my parents the schoolmaster had sent a message saying he wanted to see them when school finished. Neb told his parents the same. Of course, he was at school today.

'The master's probably missing the produce he got in exchange for your schooling,' Father grumbled. 'I won't go back on what I said. You've had enough schooling. You can read and write and you can add and take away numbers.'

'But will you go and see him?' I asked.

'I suppose so.'

I was really twitchy by the time we left. At school, we found Neb hopping anxiously outside, just as twitchy.

'What's going on?' Father demanded, when Uncle Mose and Aunt Meryt appeared.

Mother grabbed his arm. 'Don't start.'

Aunt Meryt said, "Scuse, please. The master wants to see us.'

Mother said, 'Sorry, but he –'

'No, he doesn't,' Neb and I said together.

They stared at us.

I took a deep breath. 'We think you should talk about your quarrel and sort it out. It's bad for families not to be friends.'

Aunt Meryt spoke first. 'We can't discuss this in public. You'd better come to our house.'

The men hesitated, but Mother took Father's arm again. 'Come along, Pepy.'

It was odd to be in Neb's house. It was a lot like ours, but tidier.

The men started as soon as we got inside.

'He took it!' shouted Father. 'It was mine! Our grandfather gave it to me!'

Uncle Mose snorted. 'I did not! It was mine! Grandfather gave it to *me*!'

Aunt Meryt stared at the ceiling, and Mother put her head in her hands. The little ones sucked their thumbs.

'We were in your house after Grandfather's funeral,' said Uncle Mose to Father, 'looking at the things he'd left us. Mine was in a small pouch. Weeks later, I looked in the pouch and it was empty.'

Father clenched his fists. 'And when you came accusing me, I got out my pouch, and that was empty!'

Aunt Meryt threw her hands in the air. 'All this over a couple of scarabs hardly big enough to see!'

Whoa!

'Scarabs?' I said. 'What were they like?'

Uncle Mose glared at Father. 'Mine was lapis lazuli.'

'Mine was turquoise,' said Father.

They pointed at each other and spoke together. 'He stole it!'

Neb and I instantly had the same thought. We fled from the house, through the streets, up

the hill, straight to our cave. When we got there,
we were too puffed to speak.

 We scraped and scrabbled, pulled
the box open and each grabbed a
scarab. Then we ran all the way back.

Aunt Meryt had poured beer for
everyone, and Tiya and Baba were
stuffing honey cakes. The men looked

129

everywhere but at each other. The air felt thick.

'Here.' I handed the scarab to Father.

'Here.' Neb gave the other to Uncle Mose.

Neb nudged me and I followed him into their little garden. He pushed some ducks off a pile of straw and we sat down. Immediately we heard raised voices again.

'This isn't mine! You've got mine! You stole it!'

'I didn't! You stole mine!'

We went back in to find Uncle Mose and

Father each holding out a scarab and accusing the other of stealing theirs. I went up to Father, took the lapis scarab from his hand and put it in Uncle Mose's. Then I took the turquoise one from Uncle Mose and put it in Father's hand.

'That problem's solved,' I said. 'What's next?'

I half expected to have both ears boxed but, instead, Father and Uncle Mose laughed! When they fell into each other's arms and hugged, Mother and Aunt Meryt burst into tears!

'A feast!' cried Uncle Mose. 'Our family's together again! A celebration!'

Father had a job for me and Neb. 'Go to the farm. Fetch a fine plump chicken and some of Wadj's wine!'

I must admit that when I chose a chicken, it did cross my mind to take Nasty. 'Go on,' said Neb.

I shook my head. 'A true farmer wouldn't eat a healthy male bird,' I said. True farmer? Hah! The truth is I was too scared to pick Nasty up!

When we got back, we sat outside for a bit. Eventually Aunt Meryt called us. The glorious smell of baked chicken filled the house.

But Uncle Mose and Father looked stern and serious. They lectured us about being deceitful, and how it's wrong to spy and trespass.

Then came a terrible blow. 'You, Neb,' said Uncle Mose, 'are no longer fit to follow in my footsteps. I do not want my son working with me any more. I cast you out of the Beautiful House!'

Neb was shocked silent. So was I. But there was worse.

'You, Seti,' said Father, 'have shown that you are not fit to follow in my footsteps. I do not want you working on my farm, upsetting my animals.'

The disgrace! I've never, in my whole life, known of anyone who was forbidden to follow in their father's footsteps. I turned away, holding back tears.

'Wait!' said Father. 'There's more.'

Pish! Now what? I glanced at Neb. He was

tearful, too.

'Pepy and I,' said Uncle Mose, 'have reached a decision – together. We are going to swap sons! Purely for work purposes, of course. From now on, Neb, you will work hard on your uncle's farm. And you, Seti, will continue your training at the Beautiful House.'

Oh, yes! What a day!

Everyone wanted to know how we got the scarabs. We couldn't tell them! We don't remember!

But Mother remembered us looking at them after Grandfather's funeral, fascinated by the jewel-like colours. She thinks we must have taken them that very day, and hidden them. 'I wonder what else you've got hidden – so you don't have to share with your brothers and sisters,' she said sternly. But her eyes smiled.

We both went red!

Now Neb and I are together whenever we want –
when we're not working. It's good. Life's good.
The only strange thing is that, even though I have
Neb now, I've started getting that all-alone-in-the-
world feeling again. Stupid.

Every day, I come home from the west bank
tired, happy and smelly, often in time to see Neb
getting animals ready for market, or struggling
with the plough. Our two families are forever

popping into each other's houses. The scarabs are being made into armlets for the men and, best of all, I can honestly say – at last – that I am a mummy maker!

I'm on our roof, gazing over the farm. The seeds have all sprouted, everything's madly growing again, and me? I couldn't care less! If only I didn't get that feeling . . . all alone . . .

[symbols]

Toby sat up and snorted, blowing carpet fluff out of his nose. 'Pish! What's happening?' he said. 'Hah! For a moment I thought it was chicken feathers! That rotten Nasty.'

He paused. Nasty?

'I've been dreaming,' Toby muttered. 'I dreamed I was Seti.' He flopped on to his bed. 'Whoo, what a dream.' Then he sniffed. Hot chocolate! He reached for it. It was hot.

Toby's thoughts whirled. If the chocolate was still hot, he couldn't have been asleep.

He ran to the door. 'Don!' he called. 'Did you

bring me more hot chocolate while I was asleep?'

'What?' Don yelled. 'Have you drunk the first one already?'

Toby closed the door quietly, and went to the mirror. 'I was Seti,' he murmured to his reflection. 'But if I wasn't asleep, then how? And *why*?'

Toby looked at the note on the back of the picture again. '"Piece it together and you'll find out who you are and when you come from,"' he read. 'Do I come from Egypt? Is Seti my ancestor?'

Slowly he turned and looked at the heap of paper scraps. 'Flipping heck,' he said. 'The family tree. All I have to do is fit the pieces together and I'll know. At last I'll know, and when people say, "Who's Toby Tucker?"

I'll say, "Me? I'm part Egyptian, and" . . .'

He turned to see if the chest was still there. It was.

'And what else? Let's see . . .'

Who will

TOBY TUCKER

be next?

He's Niko, dodging the donkey doo in Ancient Greece!

He's Titus, sludging through the sewer in Ancient Rome!

He's John Bunn, mucking about with monkeys in Tudor London!

He's Alfie Trott, picking people's pockets in Victorian London!

He's Fred Barrow, hogging all the pig swill in wartime London!

EGMONT PRESS: ETHICAL PUBLISHING

Egmont Press is about turning writers into successful authors and children into passionate readers – producing books that enrich and entertain. As a responsible children's publisher, we go even further, considering the world in which our consumers are growing up.

Safety First
Naturally, all of our books meet legal safety requirements. But we go further than this; every book with play value is tested to the highest standards – if it fails, it's back to the drawing-board.

Made Fairly
We are working to ensure that the workers involved in our supply chain – the people that make our books – are treated with fairness and respect.

Responsible Forestry
We are committed to ensuring all our papers come from environmentally and socially responsible forest sources.

For more information, please visit our website at
www.egmont.co.uk/ethicalpublishing